I0684401

The Beginning of Something Great:
Writing from the Prairies

Elsie Jean Leonhardt

with Kristi Spencer

ISBN: 978-0-9958752-0-3

DEDICATION

This book is dedicated to you, Grandma.

No matter what life threw at you, you always
taught us to jump over fences and find the pot of
gold in every situation. Your integrity, kindness
and compassion inspired everyone around you,
and now will do the same for your readers.
Thank you for being an inspiration, Grandma!
Love, Kristi

CONTENTS

Fiction

INTRODUCTION

By Kristi Spencer

Before my grandma passed away, I promised to try to get her stories published. She wanted the family to be able to enjoy them and we were both hopeful that they could also reach a larger audience. For years, this promise lay on my shoulders but I didn't know how to go about granting her final wish. At one point, I typed up her two completed short stories: "No Tears for Maggie" and "Little Boy Lost". I felt a closeness to her as I wrote the stories and wished there had been more time to talk with her about her life, her dreams and her thoughts. And then life got away from me again and the stories got pushed further down my list of things to do.

When a friend self-published, I realized it was the perfect time to take action. I decided to make the publication of my grandma's stories a priority. I found the old floppy disk, but realized I had no way of using the disc anymore, so I started back at square one retyping all the work she completed in the "Fiction Technique" correspondence course she took through the Literary Arts Branch of the Government of Alberta in 1973 (over forty years ago). Thankfully I was able to type these stories on my laptop, whereas Grandma had to use an old typewriter (the font I chose for this book most closely resembles the typewritten manuscripts she passed down to me).

I once again found myself immersed in my grandma's creativity. I was in awe of her writing ability and her creative mind and realized how much I want to follow in her footsteps. Writing can be such a therapeutic process. It can take us out of our everyday thinking patterns and transport us into the lives of fictional characters who we sometimes have control of and who sometimes have control over us. My grandma's writing transports me to when my grandmother was young and helps me to see her as a real person, not just as a grandma. My grandma put many of her hopes and dreams on hold to focus on raising a family. When her family was grown, she was able to take some time for herself and focus on what she loved: her kids, her grandkids and her writing. Unfortunately, in the prime of her life, when she was finally finding time to pursue her dreams, she was diagnosed with MS. Her life became full of many extra challenges that often prevented her from doing what she most wanted to do. She was still able to continue writing a weekly column for the local paper, which ended up spreading to at least five other weekly newspapers. Her columns were compiled into two published books.

Most weeks, when I was a kid, my family would load into the car and make the forty minute drive from Wetaskiwin to go see my grandparents at Pigeon Lake. I was always greeted with a tight squeeze and an enthusiastic "How's my girl?" before sitting at the kitchen table where Grandma would serve me her tasty raisin cookies (I've never found any others like them). She would ask me to draw her pictures or request that I play her a song on the piano. I was never an amazing pianist or artist, but Grandma was always my biggest fan and made me feel like I was capable of anything. When I expressed an interest in writing, my grandma gave me an old Commodore 64 that my grandpa had bought at auction. I never did figure out how to use the darn thing, but I dreamed of being an author every time I looked at it. When I learned that my grandma was a writer and that she had a weekly column, I was so proud! I enthusiastically asked her to come speak to my grade five class and was thrilled to show off my grandma. It is with that same sense of pride that I share with you the stories that my grandma wrote; stories that transported her back in time to happy memories and a less busy life, a time when values were strong and family was the backbone of society.

I hope that you will use the prompts at the end of most chapters to explore your own thoughts and creativity and add your ideas to her works in progress. May the work that came from my grandma's heart inspire you in your own creative endeavours.

Happy Writing!

Kristi

ABOUT THE AUTHOR

Credit: Wetaskiwin and District Museum Society
Compiled by: Sylvia Larson and Viki Ruben for
Women of the Aspenland
http://www.unlockthepast.ca/24/people/340

Sources: Don and Gloria Leonhardt, Ernie Leonhardt, Dorothy Patterson, Mary Blackmore, Marie Hauge, Dora Schmeelke, Rosemarie (Leonhardt) Creighton.

Elsie Leonhardt and her husband Victor were born of pioneering families. Victor was from the Drumheller area and Elsie from the Champion district. Her grandparents, Henry and Mary Schmeelke, her father, William and two sisters came from Fairbank, Iowa to Nanton, Alberta in 1906. Henry and William were able to buy land for their homesteads at $3.00 per acre. Her grandfather, Henry was a carpenter by trade and the original house he constructed was sturdy and of unique design to the Canadian west and is still home to family.

Elsie was born on May 30, 1923, the youngest child of Carrie [nee Dibb] and William. All her preschool and school years were spent in Champion and she graduated from the high school there. Her initial plans were to teach school but she met Victor and things changed.

Elsie and Victor were wed on November 7, 1942 and began their married life living near Drumheller on the farm where Victor's grandfather homesteaded. As well as farming for twenty-one years, Victor also operated a small strip mine from which he sold coal to the residents of Drumheller. Their seven children, one daughter and six sons were born in Drumheller and all but their youngest child attended school there.

About 1960, Victor became interested in land around Pigeon Lake and purchased some land through the Government and private sales. In 1962, the family made the decision to sell the home farm and move to a farm at Westerose, on the west side of Pigeon Lake.

Elsie and Victor quickly became involved with their community. They attended and were very involved with the Battle Lake Baptist Ecumenical Church. Elsie was the church pianist on many Sundays. She lent her helping hand to the Battle Lake Christmas concerts and was known to have taken her electric organ out at forty below zero to play. Her easy going, cheery and caring nature made visitors welcome in her home and she was always willing to help others.

In 1966, Elsie began writing for the Wetaskiwin Times as the Battle Lake Community correspondent. This eventually extended to a weekly column entitled *Beans and Buttermilk*. Her column told of her experiences growing up on the Prairies during the Depression and of stories retold of her pioneer ancestors. She was also known to write an occasional social or political commentary. Several weekly newspapers in Alberta carried this popular column at one time. Her columns were eventually compiled and published as three books also entitled *Beans and Buttermilk*.

Elsie continued to refine her writing skills. The Edmonton Journal offered a writing course through correspondence, which she took as well as attending seminars. She enrolled in a short story writing contest sponsored by the Edmonton Journal and was commended for her excellent story, "*No Tears for Maggie*". As well as writing her column, Elsie wrote poetry, the family history for <u>Trail Blazers</u>, and various other articles.

Elsie was a member of the Battle Lake Ladies Club and the Yeoford Ladies Club. The Battle Lake Ladies were formed in 1933-34. The club contributed money to the Cancer Fund and Red Cross, a trophy for the Mount Butte 4H, baseball uniforms for the school team and aided district residents who had suffered from fire or accident. Elsie wrote in an article on the Battle Lake Ladies Club which stated, "Ridiculed and scorned by men, the butt of many jokes, Ladies clubs survive and serve. The community is richer for their existence, in intangible ways too for when people work together to improve their district, they enrich their own lives and those of their families."

As Elsie's friend Dorothy Patterson explained, "She was a beautiful quilter." Another friend mentioned that until Elsie came to the community, the quilts were not finished quite right. Her knitting and crocheting were works of beauty. According to her friends, she had a good sense about her, was a great cook and hostess and had a strong sense of family. Dorothy said of Elsie, "She worked on the grandchildren having something to remember about the family."

Elsie had to retire from writing her column, *Beans and Buttermilk* in 1991 as the devastation from her long struggle with Multiple Sclerosis took its toll. She loved books and much of her time was spent reading. On Friday, November 23, 2001 after a short battle with a cancerous brain tumor, she passed away at the age of 78 years.

NO TEARS FOR MAGGIE

By Elsie Jean Leonhardt

Maggie Ramsey kept her eyes averted from the bare corner of the large room, and her mind firmly on her work. Only in the trembling of the hand that dipped hot water from the range reservoir into the enamel dishpan, was the turmoil of her feelings revealed. Two, three, four times the dipper lifted its precious load; she limited herself to the minimum required for the greasy breakfast dishes, for Joe had to carry the water up from the well near the barn. Though why she should continue to scrimp and save for his sake she couldn't quite fathom this morning – but four was enough. A brisk shake of the stove grates, two scoops of coal on the fire, an approving glance at the big pan of dough up on the warming oven, and she was ready to begin the dishes. She lifted the dishpan over into the sink under the window.

From years of habit, she paused to rest her fingers on the wide rim of the dishpan. By closing her eyes, she could imagine that the black and white rim was the keyboard of the organ in her childhood home, and she would practice the familiar scales and exercises to keep her fingers supple despite the enlarged knuckles. Abruptly she stopped, and plunged her hands into the hot soapy water.

"Oh Joe," she cried inwardly, "How could you do this to me?" The heartache she had carried

13

through the night swelled until her throat ached, but no tears came to bring relief.

The morning sun, streaming across the floor of the combination kitchen-dining-living room, pitilessly accentuated the cracks and patches in the worn linoleum. Though large, the room was cluttered with old and child-scarred furniture. There was that air of comfort and ease that a room acquires when it is loved and cared for. Red geraniums bloomed on the window sill, the curtains were crisp and white, and a bright flowered oilcloth covered the table.

"Hey Maggie." Joe Ramsay's booming voice preceded him to the door. "Them new pigs are out. Give me a hand, will ya?" He peered in the door, his twinkling brown eyes as much at variance with his gruff voice, as were the good humour lines on his weather-ruddy face. Seeing her standing motionless by the chipped enamel sink, he bellowed, "Hustle woman! Can't have them heading back home."

"Hustle yourself," she replied with asperity, but Joe was out of earshot, off at a jog towards the pasture. She shook the water from her hands and dried them on the gingham coverall apron.

As she went out, she slammed the door so hard in a burst of annoyance, that some flakes of the peeling paint fell to the wooden door-step.

As Maggie stepped away from the shelter of the frame house, the prairie wind caught at her skirt, wrapping it about her lean legs. The angularity of her gaunt figure had remained unsoftened even after the bearing of three husky boys and two plump girls, but her large frame had served her well, especially when it came to milking cows or retrieving pigs, she smiled wryly.

Motherhood had failed to soften the lines of Maggie's body, but it had brought lines of tenderness, laughter and patience to her face.

She ran through the garden to waylay the pigs, so that they wouldn't get in and root up all her fall vegetables. She had rows of carrots, turnips and parsnips designated for the children, and those beasts were *not* going to get them if she could prevent it. The girls in the city were expecting their babies in the spring and needed good country-grown vegetables through the winter.

Maggie sighed. She hadn't heard from Jean and Janet – from any of the children – for some time. She had been certain that there would be something from them today – of all days, but Joe had returned from the village post-office after train time this morning, carrying only the farm journals. Joe Jr. and Dave were probably working with the threshing crews and Brian, the youngest, would be settling in for his last year at the Agricultural College. She was proud of all of them, but today an unbearable pang of loneliness smote her. Besides, she had planned for so long to fill the gap left by the children's departure with her beloved music. Now it seemed she was to be denied even that comfort.

Eyeing, with disfavour, the sagging, crooked fences surrounding the pasture, Maggie decided that she would be very thankful when Brian returned to the farm. Anyone looking at those fences would judge their owner to be either an alcoholic, or incurably lazy, neither of which was the case. Joe was just Joe.

There wasn't a harder worker in three counties than her husband, Maggie conceded, as she crossed over into the meadow that Joe had rendered rock-free by back-breaking labour. The trouble was that he possessed a garrulous nature, and craved companionship as he worked, so he was always finding an excuse to help a neighbour.

Everyone around knew that underneath Joe's gruffness was a heart as soft as putty, so they always came to him when they needed a hand. Yes, Maggie sighed, helping neighbours with sore backs and flat wallets had always been Joe's way. But *this* time, and again Maggie felt emotion closing her throat, Joe had gone too far.

Of all their neighbours, Maggie liked Bill and Sadie Jones the least; they were always whining. It was just like Bill to come to Joe and beg him to buy their underfed pigs on the pretext that money was needed for Sadie's operation. But how could Joe have taken – *stolen* – her hard-earned money to buy those pigs? The money she had saved to buy an organ. Why couldn't it have been Jim and Thelma with a sob-story? They had an organ to sell, not pigs.

A sense of outrage gripped her anew as she stalked across the pasture and saw her husband and young Lonny Jones rounding up the runaways. Getting young pigs back in a pen, Maggie reflected, was like trying to put mercury back into a thermometer. Get them in a bunch, and one was sure to make a break for freedom; soon all ten were scattering in all directions. Now, with a squeal, one little porker darted off. Maggie moved into his path and shook her apron at him.

Joe rattled the feed bucket. "Soo-ey, soo-ey," he coaxed. Apparently a feed bucket was familiar wherever the home, for all ten made a bee-line for it and noisily followed Joe into the pen.

Leaning over the fence, Joe gloated over his purchase. "Ain't them a fine bunch, Maggie?"

"I'd much rather be looking at my organ," she replied with asperity, wondering how he could possibly consider *those* pigs fine.

"Now Maggie, I know you wanted it bad, but what good does an organ do? Pigs now, they're an investment. The market will go sky-high this winter." Joe seemed oblivious to her hurt and anger. "Besides, you haven't time to mess around with one now, with canning and garden and everythin'."

"I'd have time, if you'd look after your investment yourself," she retorted, stalking off toward the house.

As she opened the door, the wall telephone jangled its party-line ring. "One long, two shorts, one long," she counted and sighed. "Thelma, I reckon. I had hoped the decision might wait, but then what difference does it make, now or later."

"Hello?" She spoke into the mouthpiece extending on a swivel from the wooden box of the phone. "Yes Thelma, I was going to call you about the organ."(Click, click. *There's two rubbering on the line,* she counted.) "Well I don't know," she hesitated, then the words tumbled out. "Could you hold it for a little while? A month or two? Something's come up.

I'm sure I could have the money then." (Click, click, click went the receivers. *Most of the line must be listening in now,* she fumed.)

"Yes, I see," she answered after a long pause. "Yes – well better let the Joneses have it then. I'm sorry too. Good-bye Thelma."

She sat down heavily in the cushioned rocker. Sorry? What an understatement! She was furious. *Her* money had gone to Bill Jones for the pigs. Now Bill was the one buying the Dorins' organ. Yet he had told Joe that he needed the money for Sadie's operation! Huh!

A lifetime of practicing control over her emotions, instilled in her by stern Scottish parents in childhood, stood Maggie in good stead now. A few minutes of quiet rocking, then, "My bread," she gasped. The high white dough was almost falling over the edge of the pan. Deftly she turned it out on the floured bake table, and moulded it into neat loaves, setting them back on the warming oven to rise. She moved the heavy irons to the front of the stove. Might as well get the ironing done too, while the stove was hot.

Yesterday she had scrubbed, cleaned and polished the house in a frenzy of joy. At last she was to get an organ – the Dorin's organ. She had moved the furniture and re-arranged it so the corner would be ready for the instrument. She had chosen this special corner long ago, when Joe and the boys were building the house. "I'd like to make this room bigger, honey," he had told her then, "but this will have to do for now. And someday, me and the kids are going to get you the biggest and purtiest sounding organ ever made, Maggie. You'll see."

She had dreamed of her organ for so long, but there was always machinery to buy, or cattle, or a bull – always something to delay her dream. Then as the children grew up and left home, she found that at last she could begin to save; a few pennies here, a dollar there. Eggs brought little, but her excellent angel food cakes found a ready market at the little store and service station where tourists stopped for gas and souvenirs. Then she started selling fat brown doughnuts and sugar cookies. On real busy weekends she had even taken freshly fried spring chicken over in carefully wrapped boxes. During the winter she had done housecleaning for the town ladies; when music was concerned, Maggie Ramsay could lower her pride to do any honest work.

Her organ fund had grown steadily, but little financial emergencies drew from it often enough to dampen her hopes. To overcome discouragement at such times, Maggie pored over the descriptions of organs in the catalogue, and read avidly the classified ads in the farm papers. Then, last week word came that Thelma and Jim Dorin were selling their organ. Their girls had gone to work in the city and Thelma had never learned to play it. Besides, she wanted new linoleum for the kitchen. Her heart pounding in her throat, Maggie had hurried over to inquire about the price.

She had just enough money saved! That organ could be hers, and Joe and Jim could truck it over tomorrow evening. Last night, weary of body but jubilant in spirit, she had lifted the huge old silver bowl down from the shelf in the bedroom closet, to count again that precious horde - not copper, silver and paper, but music.

It lifted easily - too easily! Empty! It can't be empty! She peered in. A few pennies rattled about in the bottom as if to mock her. Panic gripped her - then slow realization. Only Joe knew that she had that money - and Joe had brought those pigs home this afternoon.

Clutching the bowl to her leaden heart, she had returned to the kitchen where her husband was pulling off his boots and socks.

"Joe? Where did you get the money for the pigs?" Even as she spoke she knew the answer; read it in his sheepishness, his blustering.

Now as she passed the heavy hot iron back and forth over the dampened clothing making her print dresses and aprons and Joe's shirts, satin smooth, Maggie wondered if perhaps the leaden feeling inside her might not ease if the tears would come, but tears never came easily to her. It was somehow much easier to let a laugh mask her feelings; but this time she couldn't laugh either – not yet. "Well, reckon all I can do is start saving all over again," she told the four walls, as she folded the last flannel work shirt, and set the iron back on the stove. Joy, today, had fled from Maggie Ramsay.

When Joe came in for supper, she dished up the food listlessly. He finished the last bite of pie, mopped his plate with a slice of fresh bread and ate it with gusto. Tilting his chair back on its reinforced legs he mentioned casually as he filled his pipe, "Saw Granny Marr this morning. She don't look too good. Think maybe we should take a walk over there this evening to look in on her?"

Maggie roused from her lethargy in alarm. Although the old lady was prone to attacks of illness, she insisted on living in her own home. She was a dear and Maggie loved her. "Oh Joe," she chided. "Why didn't you tell me earlier today? We'd better go right now."

"Oh, no big rush," he answered easily. "Give a guy a chance to digest that good supper." Then, "I'll give ya a hand with those dishes."

Despite her day of resentment, she was touched by his unwonted thoughtfulness. Joe had never offered to help her with the dishes before; but then again, he was probably just feeling guilty.

They did the dishes in silence, she hung up the pan, and gave a final touch-up to the already tidy room. Removing her apron and running a comb through the stiff curls of her iron-grey hair, she announced that she was ready.

"Better put on a sweater, air's a mite cool." Joe slapped his cap on and they stepped out into the September twilight. The walk across the field with the stars appearing one by one and the reflected glory of a prairie sunset still tinting the sky, soothed Maggie.

They found Granny Marr rocking contentedly as she listened to "Fibber McGee and Molly" and neither looking nor acting like she was under the weather. Baffled, Maggie looked at Joe for enlightenment, but he had joined Granny in a mutual enjoyment of "Fibber's" current dilemma. When the program ended, he opened the floodgates of Granny's reminiscences by asking her about this former neighbour or that one.

Maggie was bone-weary; she had slept little the night before and had worked hard all day. Now that her concern for Granny appeared unwarranted, she longed to go home; but Joe seemed bent on ignoring all her hints to leave. He had taken a rocking chair near the window, and seemed more interested in looking out towards home than in taking part in conversation. Of course, once Granny got started, there was little chance for anyone else to say much and Joe was probably worrying about his blessed pigs. When Grann's wheezy old clock struck nine, Maggie managed to break Joe away by suggesting that it was the old lady's bedtime.

The return path was lit by a full moon. Maggie could never resist the soft beauty of moonlight. As they neared the house she thought, once or twice, that she caught a glimpse of light in the kitchen window, but dismissed it as a reflection of the moon.

"Go on in Joe," she said. "I'm going to stay out for awhile."

He seemed about to argue, then shrugged. "Okay Maggie, suit yourself. Don't be out too long though, eh?"

She walked slowly toward the big poplar tree which they had planted as a tiny sapling on their wedding day. They had celebrated occasions each year by planting trees. When each child was born, Joe had planted twenty in its honour, a different variety for each child. Now they had a good shelterbelt around the buildings, and an assortment of shrubs. Some had not withstood the harsh prairie climate, but most had grown strong and sturdy - like the children. She lifted her face to the stars. "Oh Lord," she whispered, "how much You have blessed me; I have good eyesight and hearing, a strong body, a good home - and a good husband. What right have I to begrudge Joe my money?" Resting her head against the rough bark for a few more minutes, she gazed at the night's beauty, and peace settled over her.

Joe could have lit the lamp, she thought, walking up the path to the house, but perhaps he had decided to undress in the dark rather than to bother. She came in quietly so as not to disturb him. But in the moonlight of the room she saw Joe sitting at the kitchen table.

"Why didn't you light the lamp if you were going to sit here?" she chided gently as she reached for the matches on the shelf behind him. It was then that she saw her empty silver bowl there on the table. Ah Joe, she thought, somewhat puzzled.

He reached up and caught her hand. "Leave the lamp for now, Maggie." He drew her down to his knee. With his free hand Joe lifted the lid of the silver bowl for her to see inside. There, just as if it had never been out of the bowl, was her organ money – the dollar bills in flats of ten, the fives with an elastic band around them, the few tens held by a paper clip, and the silver strewn over all.

She looked at Joe in utter bewilderment. Even in the dim light she couldn't mistake the puckish twinkle in his eyes.

"Not a cent of it was spent on pigs," chuckled Joe.

"Then why would you pretend…" began Maggie.

A stifled giggle and a rush of feet from the bedroom brought Maggie to hers. The children were home! Joe Jr. and Dave, Janet and Jean and their husbands, and tall young Brian, all surrounded her, engulfing her in embraces.

"Happy Birthday Mother, surprise, surprise!" they were shouting.

"You kids," she said lovingly, feeling flushed with happiness.

Joe had lit the Coleman lamp and was pumping air into it, and as its brilliant light spread over the room, Maggie's eyes fell upon the *real* surprise. There in the bare corner – her heartache corner – was an organ. Not the Dorin's organ, but one that was shining new. With a gasp of joy Maggie moved towards it, fearful that it might disappear as miraculously as it had come. As the family gathered around, she caressed the satin-smooth wood, the scrollwork, the red velvet inset.

"We said we'd get you one someday, mother," said her first-born. "And then…"

"Then," interrupted Joe, "you almost spoiled the kids' birthday plans by buying the Dorin's second-hand one."

Maggie's eyes widened with comprehension. "So that's why you took my money." She gave a dismayed laugh, remembering. "Poor Joe."

"And Lord how it hurt to have you think I took it," said Joe gruffly. "That, plus letting you think we'd forgotten today was your birthday."

How long ago that misery seemed, thought Maggie, as she sat on the stool, reviewing the stops. At last she let her trembling fingers touch the keys. Was it all a dream? And would she awaken to find only the old dishpan rim beneath her fingers? She began to push the pedals with her feet. Hesitatingly, shyly, Maggie played a wisp of melody - and then another. Suddenly her fingers became alive and all unbidden they were skimming and darting among the keys bringing forth rich glorious music.

Then Maggie - the one who never would, never could shed a tear - Maggie wept.

LITTLE BOY LOST

By Elsie Leonhardt

As Beth Winters began her washing at sunrise that April morning, there was nothing to presage the anguish sunset would bring.

Their future seemed as bright as the spring outside the cabin door. She and Jason were young, strong and healthy. They had three year old Roddy, and a baby would soon be born. Another boy, Jason predicted, to help them farm the acres they were snatching from the bush.

Whistling a gay tune, Jason picked up his axe and started out the door. Pausing on the step, he called, "Hey Bets, old Matilda's back again."

The cranky old she-bear looked derisively down at them, from her vantage point on the hill back of the cabin, then ambled back into the timber.

"No Bruno," Jason shook his head at the big collie who stood beside him, bristled and growling deep in his throat, ready to give chase. "You watch Roddy. Hear? Watch Roddy." The dog accepted his orders with a quick slap of his tail on Jason's leg. "Bye Hun. Take care of my boys." A grin creased his weathered young face, and he set off with the big team of horses and the stone-boat.

Beth watched rather wistfully as they disappeared down the winding lane, then squared her shoulders and returned to her wash tub and the piles of dirty clothing which lay waiting for her. She would get these finished and have a good hot dinner ready for him when he returned at noon.

The young mother sang and told stories to Roddy as she bent over the scrub board. At noon she took the last basket of clothes out to hang up – and returned to find Roddy and Bruno gone.

Terror gripped her. The child inside moved vigorously in protest to the pounding heart above it. They can't have gone very far she reasoned, pressing her hands to her fluctuating sides.

"Ro-oddy. Bru-no." The high, thin voice lifted above the clearing.

"Ooo-no," echoed back from the tree covered hill.

Beth ran into the cabin searching every possible – and impossible – place a small boy might hide. Nothing. Outside again; another quick searching look around. Heavy-footed she ran to the log barn, looked in, and under the mangers. Roddy had once crawled into one and had fallen asleep while the big horses munched hay around him.

She clambered up the ladder to the loft and pushed her bulky body through the opening. Cobwebs dangled from the beams and glistened in the sunlight streaming through the cracks of the slab roof. Dust and bits of hay spread across the floor, but the bales had all been used through the winter and there was no place a little boy might be hidden.

The pig-pen! The cranky old sow! But no, Bruno would have been there and wouldn't let the pig touch the lad. Nevertheless, she had to look – anything to be doing *something*. The old sow lay grunting contentedly in the sunshine, The young pigs pulling and tugging at her massive belly.

"Ro-oddy? Bruno?" She called again and again, but only the echo of her frantic fear returned to her. Even the chattering birds seemed to fall silent. South of the clearing, beyond the rutted lane, was the slough filled to overflowing with the spring run-off. Beth shaded her eyes with a shaking hand as she looked for the two figures. Would Roddy have gone that way looking for his Daddy? Could he have fallen in? No, Bruno would've forestalled that. In spite of her fear, Beth had to laugh a little, recalling the commotion she had heard outside a few days ago. Roddy had been screaming in frustration, and Bruno growling. She had rushed out to find the big collie gripping the little boy by the seat of his sturdy jeans with his teeth, refusing to let him enter a deep puddle that Rod wanted to play in. No, Bruno would not let Roddy go to the slough. But where *were* they?

Roddy must then have gone up the trail. Beth looked around, with sinking heart, to the north, and the densely wooded hill.

The short-cut to her mother's cabin lay in that direction. It was also the old bear's territory in spring – and Old Matilda had been up there a few hours ago. "Oh, Dear God, no," moaned Beth as she leaned against the cabin for support. Then the rattle of harness, the clop of horses' feet, the scr-rudge of the stone-boat over the rough ground and Jason's gay whistle carried up to her. Beth ran heavily to meet him.

"Jason, is Roddy with you?" the words were wrung from her despite the evidence of her eyes that the child was not with his father.

Alarmed, as much by her distraught appearance as at her words, Jason caught her in his arms and held her tightly.

"Come, Beth, this is no good for you right now. Tell me, what's this all about?"

She drew strength from his embrace and calm voice and tried to tell him the events of the previous half hour.

"Get on the phone," Jason ordered when she paused. "Call Ma first. Ask if Roddy is there. Shush," he soothed her. "Keep your head now and try not to alarm her – remember her weak heart. Try to find out if the lad is there without letting her know you're worried. If he isn't, then phone Martha Smith and ask her if she can send some men down – they should be at dinner now." After a pause, he reluctantly added, "Maybe – better phone Big John too, at the mill. See if he can spare a few men."

Suddenly Beth knew that despite his calm manner, Jason was as frantic as she was, for Jason heartily disliked Big John. He could have had a good job at the mill, but preferred to struggle along on his own acres than work under John McLellen. The man was honest and fair, Jason conceded, but cold and ruthless in his drive for success, and they had had "words" on several occasions; the latest, when Jason had refused to let the mill boss take any trees from his land.

Jason avoided his wife's eyes as he said, "Go phone, Honey, and stay close by the house in case Roddy comes in.

Beth returned to the log cabin and Jason quickly dropped the stone-boat hitch. With a slap of the reins he set Babe and Jess at a trot for the barn.

"Thank God for the phone," thought Beth as she turned the crank on the side of the big wooden box phone; two short rings once, then again.

"Hello?" Ma Davis's voice came faintly over the wire.

"Ma?" Beth searched carefully for the right words.

"Beth? Anything wrong? Is the baby coming? I can come over and look after Roddy for you. Ralph is here and he could drive you to the hospital. Don't wait too long."

Beth was intensely grateful for her mother's volubility on this occasion, for her question had been answered before she had had to ask it. "No Ma, I'm all right, just tired." She feared then, that her mother might hear of her little grandson's disappearance by chance, once searchers were called in, so she said, "I just wanted a visit with you. Could Ralph bring you over? I'm a mite lonely."

Beth's widowed mother lived with her only son, a mile distant by a trail through the timber, though the cabin was four miles around by the road. The bush trail that they usually used, wound around marshy sloughs, passed through sections of densely wooded areas and crossed some grassy meadows. It was intersected by other trails made at one time by Crees, but now used by deer, elk and moose - and Matilda and her cubs. It was a beautiful walk in summer and fall, and easy for an adult to follow. Roddy loved to visit "Gramma" but always wanted to explore these side trails with Bruno, and had to be firmly restrained in these attempts.

On the next call, Martha Smith's brisk voice came across the bush telephone. "Martha, Roddy's lost," Beth fought to control her voice. "I'm afraid he tried to go up the trail to Ma's. And Martha - Old Matilda's back. We saw her this morning." Sobs shook her. "Could you get the men to come down? As many as possible?"

"You bet," came the brisk no-nonsense reply. "Now Beth, you get hold of yourself. He's likely close by, and he's got Bruno. He'll be ok, but we'll come over in a jacksniff. Lucky you caught us at dinner. Get the coffee pot on girl, you know these men." Click went the receiver. Martha didn't waste words. She was a woman to depend on.

The mill - she must phone the mill, much as she dreaded to. Again, she turned the crank: one, two, three short rings. This time it was the brusque cold voice of Big John McLellen, the lumber mill boss that answered her.

"Please, Mr. McLellen, could you spare some of your men this afternoon? This is Mrs. Winters. Our little boy is missing. We need help to search the bush for him."

Local gossip said that Big John was a woman hater although no one knew much about him. He was a woodsman and had opened up a large area with his lumber mills, so knew the whole area like the back of his hand. He lived alone, shunned social gatherings and was known to be very biting in his comments. Only Beth's desperation induced her to call him now. She expected him to blame her for her carelessness in letting Rod get lost; but, oddly enough, when the answer came, it was – for him – amazingly civil and full of questions.

"How old is the boy? How long has he been gone? Have you checked all the outbuildings? Small boys do crawl into odd corners."

"How would *he* know?" thought Beth.

"Where's your husband? Still out hacking a few acres?" Oh yes, there came the sarcasm, but Beth bit her tongue.

"Please Mr. McLellen, if you can spare some men would you send them over?" Then, surprised at her old boldness, she added, "I wish you could come yourself. You know this whole area, and you could organize search parties so much better." She hung up quickly before he could reply to this.

The fire was low. She needed to get wood in – and water from the well. The wash water had to be emptied. Had it only been an hour since she had finished the clothes? Must keep busy. Must not think of her little curly haired boy with a red shirt and blue trousers – her little boy with freckles on a slightly turned-up nose and a grin to twist your heart; her little boy being mauled by a bear.

Before she had the second armful of wood in the wood box, and while the first sticks were starting to blaze on the rekindled fire, Beth heard the roar and rattle of trucks on their rough winding lane that branched off the lumber road. Running to the door, she saw men jumping off the truck deck even before it stopped. Jason came running to meet them from the bush where he had done some preliminary scouting. The second mill truck had pulled up behind the first. Beth gasped. Big John was in the first vehicle; he must have closed down the mill and brought his entire crew. He stood little taller than the men grouped about him but there was a quiet strength and authority about him that had earned him the name "Big John". Eric Johnson, his foreman, stood at his elbow. Other vehicles were coming up the lane; farm wagons and "lizzies" held together by hay-wire and prayers.

Women were coming into the house laden with huge loaves of bread, wedges of cheese, hams and a roast beef, jars of pickles, pies that must have been on the tables as the men jumped into action. All had participated in searches of this nature before; no one treated it lightly. One of the women carried on her lined face the story of just such a search in this virgin territory – and the unsuccessful outcome of it.

The women immediately set to work; some made sandwiches, one fetched water, another emptied the wash tubs, and another brought in the drying clothes and started the ironing. Some pots of coffee and tea were ready and piles of sandwiches awaited the men.

Into the centre of this activity stepped Mrs. Davis. "Beth, what in the world is going on?" she queried in utter bewilderment.

"Oh Ma," Beth's control broke. "Roddy's gone, Ma. We think he tried to go up to your place by the trail. You know he always begs to. We've warned him over and over never to go by himself but he was so bored this morning – and it's such a tempting day. I went out to hang up the clothes – and oh Ma, when I came in he was gone. And it's all my fault." Her voice broke on a storm of sobs.

Mrs. Davis cradled her daughter's head on her shoulder, and looked across it at the sober faces of the other women as she sought words to comfort the young mother.

"Now Beth, don't blame yourself. Children will be children, and you've got another life to think of. The men will find him. There are more coming all the time. The word sure flies around here when folks are in trouble and help is needed. Look out there. Would you believe so many could get here so quickly?"

The men had broken into organized groups and were moving in a semi-circle toward the bush to the north and east of the clearing. Suddenly Beth didn't need to be reminded of the new babe. It announced not only its presence, but its determination to make an arrival yet that day. The familiar pain knifed through the mother. She sank into the nearest chair, very white. Martha caught the movement and asked, "Beth, you all right?"

As the pain released its hold, Beth nodded weakly. "Just a stitch in my side," she answered, but she knew better. So did Martha, and she watched closely with one eye on the clock on the shelf, as Beth caught her breath and clutched her body at regular intervals.

"We should try to get you over to the mill hospital," Martha urged when the pains were obviously coming very frequently. "We can get the next man that comes in for coffee to drive you over - and hope that's soon," she concluded under her breath.

"No!" Beth was adamant. "I'm not leaving - not with Roddy somewhere out there. Ma has midwifed. So has Mrs. Potter."

"Course I have," Annie Potter answered briskly. "Brought in maybe twenty – thirty – young'uns around these parts before Big John set up the mill hospital and even go over there to help when Doc is out on a trip. You keep walking girl while your Ma and I get things ready. Suzy Jane," she called to her granddaughter, "you skip over home and get my bag from my closet. You allus tryin' to snoop into it anyway. Don't touch nothin' in it. Just git back her real quick. Scoot," she gave the girl a push.

For Beth, the afternoon crawled by on surges of torment: physical and emotional. The men came and went, stopping in for steaming cups of coffee and large, filling sandwiches whenever the search brought them near the clearing.

Once, as she paused in one of her many walks to the open door, Beth heard one man say to another, "Matilda's tracks are everywhere. Where *is* the dog? Why doesn't he bark if he's still..." they broke off abruptly as they saw her standing just inside. She noted the quick shake of the head as the men looked at the women, and her heart sank within her.

Jason didn't come in until evening; his face gaunt and his eyes haunted. He seemed unaware of those about him or what he ate or drank. Only when he sat for a while with Beth and tried to ease her pain, did he try to conceal his discouragement. Then as the men began to light lanterns and check hand torches, he left her in other hands, and again took up the search.

Beth lay tossing on her bed then, mercifully unaware of the dusk and the lanterns moving out through the bush. She gripped Martha's strong arms in frantic grip as the babe inched its way down the birth passage. Ma Davis and Annie Parker stood by encouraging her, ready for the birth. The other women, who could stay, sat in the kitchen talking low amongst themselves, keeping the coffee pot filled and drinking cup after cup of strong hot tea as they recalled their own birthings in the ancient way of womanhood. Throughout the wood, lanterns and flashlights bobbed and men called back and forth to each other. Big John and Eric were far up the trail beyond the others. Big John was as taciturn as Eric was voluble. So it was Eric then who told the story of the next half hour repeatedly that night; and it was his version that was passed down the years, around many a fireside when tales were being retold.

"I'd give up finding the lad alive," he would begin, "but Big John wasn't givin' up so I'd stay with him. He seemed to be seeing somethin' because he stopped every few steps and held the lantern close to the ground. I couldn't see nothin' but the boss was part Injun I was heard, and I could most believe it. There was a clear sky and a full moon was rising. There would be a sharp frost that night. What chance was there for a little feller out in that wood, in a thin jacket, and with all kinds of varmints around. And what would that little mother do? Just didn't feel I could face her.

"'There's lots more kids,' Big John says. 'Goin' to be another one pretty soon or I miss my guess. She'll forget soon enough,' he grunted.

"Thinkin' of that big-eyed mother, I saw red. 'You ever had a son?' I yelled.

"'Shush up!' Big John cut me off. 'What's that sound?'

"Just a bird, I figgers, but Boss suddenly steps off to one side into a thicket and lets out a groan. I jumps after him and by the light

35

of his lantern, sees the dog, all slashed and his eyes open and glazed. Old Matilda had got him but he'd put up some fight! Then, as Boss moves the lantern, we sees the lad lying across Bruno's flank — alive. Big John had heard his cry; I'd have missed it. In one stride he was there and running his big hands gently over the boy checking for injuries. At the touch of those hands the little feller sat up and looked at the boss with a big smile.

"'Are you Jesus?' he asks. 'Mommy says Jesus finds his lost lambs, and you finded me.'

"Well sir, the Shepherd was sure looking after this lamb; the old bear had ripped the dog open and never touched the lad. He had lay on his dog and cried hisself to sleep.

"Ya know, in all the time I worked for Big John McLellen, I seldom heard him laugh — but he did then. And he lifted that lad in his arms like he would a hurt animal and began croonin' to him — tough Big John!

"I grabbed the gun and ran down the trail to fire the signal shots that the boy was found, but I tell ya, I could hardly see, my eyes were so full o' tears.

"When we gets near the clearing I remembers what I asked the boss, and I asks him agin, but not mad this time.

"'Hey Boss,' I says, 'you ever have a son?'

"I didn't think he was goin' to answer, then he says, 'Aye.'

"'Well,' I says, 'what happened to him?' None of us ever hear tell of a son — or a wife either for that matter.

"Then Big John says, like the words were drug out of him. 'Name was John – like mine. He was about the age of this lad. Wandered off one day when his Ma was crying her eyes out cause she wanted to go back east. He didn't get far, but the woods was so thick in them days, that when we found him he was dead. Well, the woman said she was leaving and couldn't say I cared much now the lad was gone. The woods was my life; always had been – always will be, I reckon, but the boy gave meaning to it. Would have brought him up to love it too.'

"Yep, you never can tell from the outside, what a man can be carrying inside him – or what might bring it all out," concluded Eric.

Beth was wrapped in a blanket of peace and joy. One son lay snuggled against her breast, his great journey safely accomplished; he was content. Roddy leaned from the arms of Big John, his eyes full of wonder at the sight of the tiny babe; his adventure also ending safely. Then he wound his chubby arms around the big man and nestled his head on the broad shoulder of his rescuer.

"How can we ever thank you?" Beth and Jason spoke as one voice.

"Everybody was doing his share," Big John shrugged. "I was just lucky," then the rare smile crossed his lips, "but if you really want to thank me…" Jason braced himself, prepared to lose his best timber to the McLellen mill - but Roddy was worth every log on the place. "Maybe," the mill boss continued, "you can let me get this lad another collie. And would you let the boy come with me sometimes so I could teach him about the woods? Since he's so fond of them. Seems he's kind of fond of me too."

Big John McLellen broke into a wide grin as he gently laid Roddy into the arms of his astounded father and quietly stepped out into the night.

My "Grandparents"

By Elsie Jean Leonhardt

I was the youngest in our family, but grew up shy and timid. When I was about sixteen, an elderly couple, old family friends, needed a girl to help out and asked for me.

The wife had suffered a stroke several years previously and was bedridden. They loved young people and counted my sister and me among their grandchildren. As we had never known our own grandparents, we were glad to adopt Grandma and Grandpa Dole as our own. Even though the stroke had badly crippled her, Grandma was so happy natured and patient, that friends flocked to her bedside. I loved the Doles dearly but I especially adored their youngest daughter, Lella.

One time when I went to the Dole's as nurse companion to Grandma, the normally placid river that ran past the foothills town where they lived was a torrent; swollen by the melting of an unusually heavy snowfall in the mountains that spring. I had never seen a river in flood but I was due to make a terrifying acquaintance with one.

When the river rolled over its banks and into town, friends rushed over. They helped Grandma get out into a waiting ambulance and it had hardly pulled away when the first waters of the rampaging river were lapping at its tires.

I'll never forget the horrible sensation as water poured into the basement and rapidly filled it. When it started rising on the main floor, Grandpa and I took to the second floor where we watched it rise step by step. When it halted at the two foot level, we knew we were safe. There were cooking facilities up there, along with our bedrooms and bathroom. Thankfully, power and sewer continued to give service.

That night, alone in my room, I turned from side to side. With the horror of that black water gurgling and swirling around in the house, I couldn't sleep. Suddenly, the telephone rang, echoing hollowly throughout the main floor where it was located. Stark terror gripped me. Grandpa couldn't answer it, he was quite deaf. It was probably Aunt Lella who lived out of town. Hearing of the flood, she would be frantic about her parents.

I had to answer that phone, so I went to the bend of the stairs and looked down at the murky water dimly visible from the street lights outside. While I didn't feel I could go down into it, I knew I must. Step by step, I forced myself down into the icy water, working my way over to the phone. Through teeth chattering as much from fear as cold, I reassured Aunt Lella as to the safety of her parents.

I was to repeat that trip several times more that night, as worried friends kept calling, but that first one was the worst.

Our own experiences can often become great stories. Think of a time in your life when you overcame an obstacle. Use your writing to convey the feelings and thoughts related to the experience.

What's in it for Me?

By Elsie Jean Leonhardt

Why am I taking this course in fiction technique? I can answer this questions best by using an idiom of my background. Why does a gardener use fertilizer on his garden? You can start with good soil, seeds, moisture and lots of hard work, yet still achieve only mediocre results from your backyard garden. Add the proper fertilizer and you can produce a sturdy, well-balanced plant worthy of the effort.

There are writers who have the soil, the seed and good growing conditions; who certainly do plenty of hard work and who produce works of excellence. For me, however, a fascination with words and a depth of feeling were insufficient to produce satisfactory results, even with lots of ideas running around in my head. I needed a basic knowledge of the ground rules in writing creatively, plus qualified criticism and to gain confidence in what I'm doing.

I have read avidly from the time I could put letters together to form words. Books, to me, are doors to other realms. They are a panacea when I am depressed, discouraged or unable to sleep. At these times I don't want a book filled with bitterness, cynicism, satire or sex, though these subjects have their place and time. I seek, rather, books of love, courage and inspiration.

There is a multitude of books on the market today, many of which leave me feeling depressed, disgusted and degraded in some way. I resent having my face rubbed in a manure pile when there are roses blooming along the way.

I want to write creatively, but not flauntingly. There is much beauty, heroism, decency and just plain "goodness" in the world around us and I am naive enough to feel people want, and need, to read about it. They need to be reminded of their roots in the soil and of those hardy pioneers who settled this land. In China, ancestors are worshipped; we should at least have a nodding acquaintance with ours. There are already authors with this thought in mind; I'd like to at least attempt to join their ranks.

I don't really desire fame; it might be all right, but very hard to live up to. Nor do I particularly desire to make a fortune, which is a good thing as I don't really see myself doing so. There is, however, an immense feeling of satisfaction in earning money by your own creativity and hard work. I'd like to earn enough to live simply but comfortably, and I'm idealistic enough to want my work to be of a high moral standard. To attract readers so that they live with the characters I have created until the last page, then feel better for having done so is, to me, a satisfaction.

If some work of mine brings courage to someone, happiness or laughter to others; if it renews faith in someone who is wallowing in the depths of despair, I would feel this more worthwhile than fame or fortune.

So this is my aim. What do I hope to get out of this course? In rereading things I have written, I feel some have merit. Would others find them readable? Some of my stories definitely have something lacking. In what way? How can I improve them? I need a much greater knowledge of writing. Where can I find a qualified critic, someone who knows writing and doesn't know me personally? Enrolment in this course has brought me many of the answers I was seeking. In the corrections and suggestions, I find that often it is little things: the turn of a phrase, the rephrasing of a sentence, or a change in ideas that can turn an inept work into an intriguing one.

I am learning to observe, to probe, to question and to understand myself and others better. Though I have no illusions that this course (or any other) is going to provide a magic vitamin pill that will provide instant and guaranteed success, it certainly will enrich the "soil" of my mind. Through cultivation, transplanting and much weeding, I do hope to produce plants that will provide wholesome food for hungry readers.

Why do you want to write? Are you writing for yourself or for others? Do you wish to entertain, inform or leave your legacy through your written work? Where do you feel you need more practice or knowledge to improve your writing ability?

Welcome to my World

By Elsie Jean Leonhardt

It has become the practice to so belittle and denigrate the role of housewife, that many young wives are out chasing career rainbows instead of looking for the pot of gold that could be found right in their own homes.

For over thirty years I have been a housewife and I can't think of any career that I would rather have had or one that would have been more fulfilling. I have been a partner in my husband's work as well as in his life and we have shared the triumphs and failures. I have borne seven children, cuddled and chastised them; watched them take their first steps, both physically and mentally, in careers and in life.

To make a good home requires more varied talents than any other career that I can think of: cook, nurse, diplomat, seamstress, interior decorator, hairdresser, barber, secretary, and on and on. In the role of housewife, you are pretty well your own boss, but total responsibility for the home and family rests squarely on your own shoulders. What you don't know (and in my case, this was a lot) is learned by the trial and error method. Though this can have sometimes devastating, often comical results, it is certainly a thorough way to learn. For example, in short courses I have known Home Economists to advocate a certain method verbatim from the book, that I had tried and discarded years before because it was impractical. A year or so later I found they too had discarded that method in favour of the one I had adopted.

Similarly, some young mothers base their whole method of raising a child on a book written by some child "authority". They ignore the fact that their own mothers had successfully raised families and had learned a few things about it in the process that might have been more practical than some of the eminent Doctor's theories. Plain common sense is, I think, the most valuable ingredient for a successful housewife; add to this enthusiasm, experience, and knowledge gleaned from others, from books and periodicals and from short courses, and you can procure a fairly well balanced education in homemaking.

There are many facets to being a homemaker. You can develop your own personal talent from any one of a dozen different routine occupations around the house. This, to me, is one of the fascinating parts of being a housewife. You can take your child for a walk and his eager curiosity can launch you into rock collecting and polishing; collecting and mounting insects; a study of wild flowers native to the area or bird-watching. Stemming from the study of nature, you can become interested in oil painting or astronomy (the sky's the limit).

Cooking is a real challenge with so much scope for imagination and experimentation. Music is an outlet, especially for those who have studied it in their youth. Starting from scratch musically, instruments and lessons are readily available. Get involved in making the children's clothes and your own in order to economize and you can get interested in dress designing. The home is an ideal place to try your own ideas of interior decorating - if you have a patient husband. Arts and crafts are an extremely fascinating project and the finished product can add much to the home.

I have just scratched the surface; volumes could be written (and probably have been) on each of the above interests. I have been involved in most of the ones mentioned, but my greatest interest has been in sewing and design, and crafts emanating from this. I taught my only daughter and several other girls and women the art of sewing. My six sons became interested and now each one can do as professional a job as most girls, and better than many. They all have excellent taste in choosing their own clothes also. My favourite hobby though (next to writing) is quilt making. There is so much scope for imagination; the quilt symbolizes "home", warmth and comfort, and can be passed down in the family, as treasured heirlooms.

The fulfillment from thirty two years as a "housewife" can perhaps be summed up as follows: to hear my children call "Mother?" whenever they arrive home and be reassured by my presence; to be missed by my husband when I'm away for a few days and to be joyfully welcomed home; to know the house is empty when I'm not in it, is to me a greater honour than laurels from strangers who might honour me today and condemn me tomorrow.

In my children (those to whom I've given birth and the ones they have chosen as mates) and in my grandchildren, my existence and influence will carry on long after I have passed on. I believe that this influence will have more far-reaching effects for good because I was the hub of the home and my love encompassed it.

Think about the various roles you hold. Make a list of all the roles you serve on a regular basis. Which role do you feel most at home in? Write about the value of this role both for yourself, your family and your larger community.

I Want a House - a Little House

By Elsie Jean Leonhardt

Despite the fact that women in earlier days spent most of their time within the confines of the home and did most (if not all) of the work within it, they were rarely consulted in the building of a home. In fact, most contractors were very antagonistic to female ideas.

From early childhood I was fascinated with house designs and floor plans. Like most women of my generation, my life was male dominated from my grandfather right down to my six sons. Though I have been fortunate in living in two new homes and have been very fond of both, ideas I had as to the construction were usually over-ruled, especially if there was conflict of ideas. So, I have a dream - of a house.

My dream house would be relatively small, but two storied, with dormer and gable windows among the ones on the main floor. The basement would be entirely in the ground so that the house would blend in with the surrounding area instead of being perched up on a pedestal of cement like a too short dress lengthened with a band of dirty grey flannel.

The basement would contain a root cellar and a food room with lots of shelves. There would, of course, be the furnace and laundry rooms, and a place for kiddy cars, toys and games in which

children of all ages could work off their
exuberance.

On the upper floor would be extra bedrooms
with large windows we could see out of; not little
peek holes stuck prison-like up under the eaves.
No, I would have windows one could sit at and gaze
far across fields and bushland; that sunlight and
moonlight could stream through and an ill person
could look out of from the bed. There would be
closets big and small, wherever one could be
placed; for storage and to intrigue little
children.

On the main floor I'd like a bedroom and
bath for the convenience of age and illness; a
kitchen modern enough for convenience and old-
fashioned enough for comfort. There should be a
dining room for family gatherings with a china
cabinet filled with precious old china, family
heirlooms, and crystal and silver. A big sturdy
table and comfortable wood and leather chairs to
surround it.

The living room would be a "living" room in
every sense of the word. I want a fireplace with
low soft chairs that cradle a tired body. There
must be bookshelves, lots of them, with old and
new favourites to fill them. The bay window must
face south, and the big shelf in its arc would be
for house plants with a cushioned corner for Pussy
to sun herself.

I must have an old fashioned veranda, glass
enclosed for the winter, screened for the summer.
Here I would have a comfortable old sofa and one
or two rocking chairs so we could sit and relax on
hot summer evenings or nap on sunny afternoons.

Around the house I would have climbing vines
and hollyhocks, with flower beds bordering the
lawn. In these I would plant tulips, peonies,
bleeding heart, delphinium for the hummingbirds,

and other old favourites. Near the house I would like a couple of big trees so that squirrels and chipmunks could chase up and around the limbs and birds could nest nearby. Underneath should be a hammock for lazy days.

Behind my dream house, what else but a vegetable garden, with a good tight fence to keep out exploring cows and other sundry farm animals. There should be a little gate however, with a good stout latch. I am very tired of climbing over or under fences.

Ah well, enough of dreaming. I must wrap up my favourite dream once more and tuck it away in the treasure chest of impractical ideas and queer notions. The Bible says, "In my Father's house are many mansions." Dear Lord, I don't want a mansion; all I want is a little house with a porch and a bay window.

As writers, we tend to spend a lot of time in our homes. Describe your dream home. Compare and contrast the dream home to the home you currently live in. What minor changes could you make to feel closer to your dream?

The Trails of Life

By Elsie Jean Leonhardt

Even with the greater portion of life lying behind me, it's not easy to single out one unrealized ambition. There are so many. In the conceit of youth, life's highway is criss-crossed with countless roads and smaller trails of opportunities, there for the taking. As responsibilities are assumed, however, we must put on blinders and thus see only the road ahead. Various by-ways are passed unnoticed and we assume that others were only mirages.

Now, with the family raised, we take the blinders off and the road branches out again and the view is more clear-cut, and seen with a realism that experience brings if we will accept it.

A university education was one of the old trails but the entry to it was barred by the ogre "Depression". It would have been helpful to have had that training, and to be able to add those very official looking letters after my name. But now I look at many people graduating from universities with a surfeit of knowledge - and so little wisdom.

Would I have been one of these, so intent with what I could learn from books that I wouldn't have had time to learn what life could teach me? There are those who are busy trying to chase every new wisp of learning that they haven't time to listen, to understand others or to feel compassion.

I would like to have much more knowledge, not of the wonders of science, space, economics or world politics, although they are very important. No, I would like to learn more of the people around me; such as the day to day experiences of that old farmer when he first set foot in this country and felled trees on his homestead. Of the experiences of that little old lady at his side, in those early days and of the country they came from and the life there.

Other paths that beckon are those leading to England. Oh, to walk in English meadows, travel the canals, visit a castle and browse through history-book England. I'd love to go on an archaeological dig and to visit with rural people in Europe, Australia and New Zealand.

Actually, the main road that connects all those is to write intelligently with understanding about what I would see and learn.

I don't think I would really class any of these as unrealized ambitions yet; not until the final curtain comes down. Even then, who knows what glories lie beyond? Since I seek knowledge and wisdom, perhaps that is where I'll find it. I hope so.

What are your unrealized ambitions? Do you have a bucket list or a grand idea that has yet to become reality. Write as if you are at the end of your life. What have you accomplished? What do you wish you had done that you didn't get a chance to realize? What would you do differently if you could start over?

*Elsie did realize her dream of traveling to Europe when she visited her son and his family in Scotland. She toured castles and walked in flowery meadows.

Shadows of History

By Elsie Jean Leonhardt

Anthony Henday travelled through this land after going as far west as the present site of Rocky Mountain House with his band of Crees. He was the first white man (as far as is known anyway) to come this far west, and somewhere along this trail he "beheld the shining mountains". I stand on the hills overlooking Battle Lake and try to visualize the scene as he saw it over two hundred years ago. The history of this small area alone fascinates me.

Somewhere along this lake shore is the site where the first Protestant missionaries west of Winnipeg, Rundle and Steinhauer, attempted to teach the Crees a knowledge of agriculture. They had hoped that by so doing, they could provide them with a more reliable standard of living. It was not to be, however, for in the absence of the Cree leaders, a band of marauders swept down on the little settlement and massacred everyone there.

Sometime in these years of petty squabbling among the tribes, there was a fierce battle between the Cree and the Blackfoot. The hill where I now stand was covered with native warriors, judging by the arrowheads found here and the valley below must have echoed to the shrieks of battle. The story is told that so many bodies fell into the lake that it was believed to be haunted by the spirits of those buried beneath the waters. Not until a recent and scoffing generation grew up, would the First Nations people fish at this end.

Down there, to my right, is some rusting machinery and an old pile of sawdust, all that remains to mark the first inroads of the white men. They came with their tools and machinery and set up camps and a store. This opened the way for the homesteader. His history can be read in that log cabin down to my left. And in this mound just behind me is a simple wooden cross and head marker. Was it the resting place of a young man coming to this wild land full of eagerness and high hopes? Was it perhaps a young mother with a babe in her arms, both lost because of no medical help? Was it an old man, who found the struggle to tame this land too much? The graves of all these are said to lie in the area.

Yes, this valley is a treasure house of Alberta history, but accurate information is getting harder to obtain with the passing of each year. The ones who first broke soil here have either passed away or now have failing health and memories. Truly, history lies at my feet.

Go to a favourite outdoor location. Who do you think walked this land before you? You can think back to the distant past or possibly to only a few moments before you arrived. What stories do you think this land has seen and heard?

Around the Bend

By Elsie Jean Leonhardt

My childhood home lay in two school districts. Dad's homestead, on which the barns and outbuildings were built, was on the east side of the road in one district. Grandfather's land, on which the family home had been built, was on the west side of the road in another school district. It was exactly the same distance to each school.

When my brother, nine years my senior, started school, the one to the west was considered "tough" so he was sent to the school to the east. My sister and I followed suit.

The first four years I was in school, we were taught by a firm and competent teacher. The next three years a young lady was hired who seemed to feel that her main duty lay within the domain of the school and the teaching of the three R's. What went on outside didn't concern her. Anything could, and did, happen out there.

I was a shy and awkward child. My chum was a cousin of the two school bullies. Her mother was in a mental institution. Whatever the reason, we were singled out for the most tormenting. We dared not complain to the teacher or at home, or even worse treatment would have been meted.

At the completion of grade eight, we rebelled. My chum went to live with her grandmother in the village to attend school there. If I was to continue school, as I was determined to do, I either had to travel the six miles to the village, or go to the country school to the west. Though I knew little about it, and my parents disapproved, I chose the latter course.

I took grades nine and ten at this school. They were difficult years academically, as we lacked many of the study aids now considered necessary. However, they turned out to be two of the happiest and most fulfilling years of my life.

Have you made a decision in your life that others have frowned upon or you felt unsure of, but it ended up being the right decision for you? What led you to needing to make a choice and why did you choose the route you did? How did it work out for you and what would you change if you could?

Miss Schultz and the Plagiarists

By Elsie Jean Leonhardt

True Story:

Miss Edith Schultz entered my life that first bewildering day in the village high school. She exuded a serenity that gave me confidence then, and throughout the three years until I graduated.

She was big of body, mind and spirit. She stood at least six feet tall and weighed well over two hundred pounds, but not one bit of it was flab. Her eyes were grey, cool and speculating, and her hair was greying but always controlled.

Miss Schultz's aim in life was to teach her pupils a love of literature and poetry. Of greater importance, she taught us to think for ourselves.

Shortly after beginning grade eleven in the village school, Miss Edith Schultz, our English teacher, gave our class an essay assignment. I can't recall that she gave any extra incentive or placed any particular stress on this assignment, but it seems she may have done.

I was always scribbling verses and stories, but somehow school assignments did little to foster creative writing.

For my essay, I chose a musical topic, The Grand Canyon Suite, with which I was quite enamoured at that time. A lot of effort went into it, and I felt proud of my effort.

The day the essay papers were to be returned to us, Miss Schultz took her stance in front of her desk. She fixed us with a steely look and delivered a lecture on the evils of plagiarism.

The essays were good, she said, but there were some seven of us who had disappointed her. Our blank looks of astonishment must have puzzled and irritated her, because there was an edge to her voice as she read out the names of the seven culprits. Mine was one of the names.

One by one we declared our innocence, and assured her of our knowledge of the subject we had chosen. I guess we convinced her.

My own effort was reproduced in the high school yearbook. I had discovered the satisfactions of "writing".

I'd like to say that we seven went on to achieve great things, but sadly enough these were our only outstanding essays that year or next. Probably the shock of being accused of something with such an imposing name as "plagiarism" put a damper on any future special efforts in this line.

Creative Writing:

Jeanine, a high school student, has an interest in writing and music. She has a "crush" on her English teacher, whom she respects and admires.

The teacher is an exacting person with high principles. She endeavours to inspire her pupils to think for themselves and then express their thoughts. To encourage this, she assigns an essay contest. The pupil may choose any topic that interests him or her. The best essay will be printed in the high school yearbook. In addition, a prize of two dollars will be given to the student who produces this essay.

Jeanine is determined to produce an essay of merit, for four reasons. She wants to please her teacher, earn the esteem of being in the yearbook, express herself in writing, and win the prize money.

Oh, to win the prize. There is a beaded sweater in the catalogue, just that price. All the girls are wearing them and this one is such a beautiful blue.

However, this is going to take time. There are farm chores to do before and after school. Just getting to school involves riding horseback to a farm on the van route, caring for the horses there, and changing into school clothes before the van comes. It means leaving home early and getting home late. There is the music lesson to practice, and the other homework to do. There is little spare time to research and write the essay.

The deadline draws closer. A book she needs has been loaned. The night she must finish is Dad's favourite night with his radio programs. She works until after midnight, gets a few hours of sleep, then gets up in the early morning hours to recheck her work. With the clarity of morning thought, she knows she has done well, but is it good enough?

The essays are handed in. A week passes, the class is expectant, some students are making confident plans to spend the money.

At last the day of the judging arrives. Instead of returning the papers however, and announcing the winner, Miss Schultz stands before them and delivers a stern lecture on the deceit of plagiarism.

Blank astonishment greets her lecture, and she becomes rather annoyed. The seven best essays, she thinks, are copied. She hasn't proof of it, she admits, but she just doesn't feel that these students can do this well.

She calls out the names and each one is given the opportunity to express his or her familiarity with their chosen subject. After grilling each one, she concedes their innocence.

Jeanine is one of the seven. Her topic on music pictures, "The Grand Canyon Suite" in particular, is chosen for the prize.

She can get the desired sweater, of course, but there is a bigger thrill out of exceeding the teacher's expectations, and of having convinced Miss Schultz that the effort is her own.

*Most authors choose to write about events that are familiar to themselves and true to life, whether from their own lives, stories they've heard from friends, or something they've seen on the news. After writing an in-depth description about a character from your real life, write a memorable story that involves that person. How can you embellish the story to make it more interesting for readers? Play around with exaggerating and changing some key elements to turn your real life story into an entertaining work of fiction. Think of some ways that the story could have turned out differently by asking yourself, "What if?" By using **what if**, you can make your story more suspenseful, more humorous or more entertaining.*

The Recipe for Love

By Elsie Jean Leonhardt

Character Sketches:

Denny McDougall

Denny is a school teacher become farm wife; had kept house for her father through her high school and teaching years in the Southern Alberta city where they lived. She met Rob while he was stationed at a nearby Air Force Base. Upon his discharge from the Air Force, they were married and came to the farm homesteaded by his parents. At first she enjoyed the novelty of farm life but now she is disillusioned by the lack of facilities in the old house, and puzzled by Rob's refusal to change things in it. She is discouraged by the daily grind of hard work, for which there seems such small return.

Denny's main grievance however, is her husband's continual praise of his mother, and her ways of doing things. No novice at cooking and housekeeping, Denny feels she should rate more appreciation for the work she does and the contribution she makes to the marriage.

A letter has come requesting her to return to her teaching of a special experimental class in the city. The recognition of her ability in this line, expressed by the supervisor of this school, bolsters her waning confidence in herself. She decides to leave Rob and the farm for the more fulfilling (she feels) teaching job.

Rob McDougall

Rob is a sensitive, quiet man, born and raised on this farm. He has a deep love of the land, which was intensified by the desecration he saw, and to which he had had to contribute as a pilot on bombing missions in Europe.

The various aspects of farming absorbed him from his first uncertain steps tagging after his father, to the two years he studied at the Agricultural College. When his father was killed in a farm accident, he and his mother carried on by themselves. He has a deep love and respect for his mother because of their common bond of love for the farm. While Rob was away at war, his mother, Amy stayed at the farm raising some livestock but renting out the land.

After Rob married Denny and brought her to the farm, Amy moved to a furnished apartment in the city, leaving the farm home essentially as it had been. Rob likes it this way and opposes Denny's efforts to modernize.

Mrs. Kessler

Mrs. Kessler is a nearby neighbour. She and her husband are an elderly couple who homesteaded when the McDougalls did, and shared with them the ups and downs of those days. She is a close friend of Amy's, not too well educated, speaks with the idiom of her time and place.

Amy McDougall

Amy enters the story only through the eyes of the other characters.

Story Outline:

The story opens on the modern farm home, and a chance remark Rob and Denny's son makes to his fiancee: "Be sure and get Mom's recipe for Chiffon Cake, can't beat it!"
(Denny putting dishes in the dishwasher, the open window brings in the scent of newly swathed grain and the clatter of the self-propelled swather in the distance, her son's voice from the patio)

Through the trees she sees the weathered old farmhouse, now used as a workshop, and her memory leaps twenty six years to her life as a newlywed living in the old farmhouse.

Flashback:

She is counting the last strikes of the wheezy old clock downstairs, eight, nine, ten. The passenger train stops briefly at the village station a mile away, at two o'clock daily. She, Denny McDougall, will be on it when it pulls out. The letter offering her the teaching position is tucked reassuringly in her pocket.

A truck loaded with bawling cattle stops in front of the house. Rob is leaving for the city stockyards and will be gone for the day. Before leaving, he tells her he will be stopping at his mother's apartment for lunch. To cover his concern for Amy, he tells Denny teasingly that he needs to get one of Mom's good meals again. Wistfully he mentions Amy's homesickness for the farm. He suggest bringing her back with him to do the cooking while he and Denny do the harvesting. Denny is shocked at the idea that she is expected to go out stooking. Rod assures her that she is strong enough and clever enough to make a stook that will stand - it's just a matter of mathematics. After all, Mom did it and she was "a little bit of a thing". Denny hears only the words, not the teasing underlying them. She's leaving. Let Rob bring his mother home. She agrees to the suggestion but keeps her own plan to leave secret from him.

In the three hours now remaining until train time, Denny tallies what she has to do. Allow a good half hour to walk across the field to the station - it's shorter and she won't meet any people. Pack a small valise - only the necessities. She'll need some new clothes to go back to school again anyway, hers are pretty shabby now. Leave the house in immaculate tidiness - Amy can't accuse her of poor housekeeping! Will she have time to bake a cake and two pies? Rob's favourites of course.

Just as she puts them in the oven and adds more coal to the stove, she looks out and sees the sheep in the test plot of wheat. Got to get them in, that new variety of wheat shows promise. She uses more precious time at this, then fixing fence.

Returning to the house she finds her neighbour, old Mrs. Kessler waiting for her. It's twelve-thirty - one hour left. She must ask the old lady in for a cup of coffee and bite of lunch. The pies and cake are done and set to cool.

As Mrs. Kessler savours her coffee and a slice of the fresh cake, she rambles on and on about the old days, and what a marvellous neighbour Amy was.

Denny panics as the minutes tick by. Just as she starts to tell the old lady that she has to leave, she is startled to hear Mrs. Kessler say, "Yep, Amy was a mighty fine person, but she sure warn't no housekeeper or cook - not like you be," and holds out her cup for a refill.

With the full cup before her, she continues, "Rob'd never say a word agin his mom, but he got so tired batchin! Amy was gone a lot helpin' other folks, or tired out workn' with the stock. He allus said when he got him a wife, he was gonna look to her cookin' first, to her looks after. Amy bragged as how he got both, a prize cook and a looker, when he got you. You're one lucky gal, got both yer man and his mum braggin' ya up," she chuckles.

Tentatively she asks Denny if she can get the "receipt" for "that new fangled chiffon cake". Had all the women at the church supper jealous.

The clock strikes two, the train whistles its departure from the station. As she pours yet another cup of coffee, and sets another piece of chiffon cake before her neighbour, Denny starts planning a gourmet supper for Rob and Amy. Perhaps helping to develop a first rate farm might be a greater challenge than teaching, now that she had the "receipt".

Strong characters are integral to a great story. Planning out a character before writing can provide direction and insight into how the character will behave and handle any obstacles or problems during the story.

A story outline contains key plot points and character motivations. It can also include phrases or dialogue that you want to make sure to include in your draft. A story outline does not have to be set in stone, but it helps to provide direction and helps to ensure you have thought about how to deal with any difficulties in plot.

Most aspiring writers have a story they want to tell. Start becoming more familiar with the characters in your story. What really makes them tick? Do they have any habits or mannerisms that make them unique and would help the reader identify with them. Make sure you write down any ideas as they come to you, no matter how small or seemingly insignificant. The more thought out your characters are, the stronger your story will be.

The next several chapters include analyses of characters and/or outlines. Use these examples as a guide when planning your own story or practice writing a short story by turning these outlines into a full story.

The Call of the Mountain

By Elsie Jean Leonhardt

Character Sketches:

Garth

Garth James was a study in contrasts. He had a rippling feline litheness while hiking and mountain climbing. In a carpeted, ornament cluttered home, he was as awkward as an adolescent.

His luminous dark eyes looked on life with the eagerness of a child, yet thirty years of wandering had shown him much of the seamy side of life.

He was tall, big-boned and loose limbed. A long lean face, smooth cheeked as a boy, straight black hair, clipped to a brush, all gave the impression of native ancestry, yet his parentage was indubitably Anglo-Saxon.

He had traveled around the world, had hob-nobbed with Sherpas in Nepal, sheep herders in Australia, a Rajah in India and a Duke in England. Mount Everest had evoked his adoration as much as the Taj Mahal. Archeology fascinated him and he had worked on "digs" in Arabia, England and the United States. He was an avid reader, his books covering a wide range of subjects; his knowledge accordingly. Despite this, he seemed in many ways as naive as a country boy. Uneducated choppers at a bush camp considered him a good target for their jokes. He was tolerant of these, and teasing at his own expense, but any slight to a friend, especially a girl, was met with flashing eyes and flying fists.

Garth had an ardent love of the mountains and the high country. This was his true home. When he travelled abroad, his favourite trips involved mountain climbing and searching out trails among the slopes.

His favourite occupations were working forest fire look-out stations, and guiding hiking groups and trail rides.

Linda

Linda Wrenkin looked as fragile as an eggshell. Belying her appearance however, all four feet eight inches of her was disciplined muscle and determination in an attractive female form.

Her eyes were the redeeming feature of a rather plain face. They were large luminous grey, rather wistful, as if yearning for far horizons.

Sun-bleached hair clipped short, told of many hours outdoors. A nose that was frankly "pug" and a rather crooked mouth, made one consider her plain, but her smile radiated a quiet loveliness.

Nature was her habitat. Five days a week she efficiently performed her secretarial duties in a cramped, smoke-filled office. On weekends and holidays however, she took to the mountain trails and slopes, hiking and skiing, breathing deeply of the fresh clean air of freedom.

She was skilled at packing her equipment, and back-packed her full share of the group camping needs on the hiking expeditions. Somehow she always ended up as camp cook, even though jobs were assigned fairly, and the more glamourous members were assigned this duty.

Roy Bartlet, Linda's "steady", accompanied her on these treks, though Linda suspected it was more because of the desire to exploit his fine physique among the female population on the slopes than any real love of the outdoors. His handsome appearance showed up much more to advantage in ski outfits than in the ordinary business suit.

However, with her deftness, Linda rolled his back-packs or tended to his ski equipment and tolerantly laughed off his many derogatory jibes at her appearance and errors. One doesn't expect a Greek god to be concerned with mundane affairs.

Story Outline:

Garth, just returned from a trip overseas, is temporarily unemployed.

An old hiking buddy who is too busy to take on any extra work, urges him to assist on a trail hike for which a group is looking for a guide. Though not too socially minded, he agrees to go. He enjoys hiking, but expects some of the group are social butterflies more intent on seeking new experiences than climbing mountain trails. He plans to set them a tough course.

Roy and Linda are in the group. At first Garth looks with disfavour on Linda. He feels she will be unable to keep up, and generally not pull her weight in the group. Besides, he is more interested in girls who are tall and striking in appearance.

Among the group, there are several girls more to Garth's taste. One of them is a stately blonde named Serena. He forgets his scruples about "social butterflies" and becomes more enthused with his job.

Roy also finds Serena to his taste and looks forward to the trip ahead. Though he expects Linda to do his work, he turns on his charm for Serena and the others.

Linda competently keeps up with the camp work and stays near the head of the line on the steep hike. Serena on the other hand, falls behind and demands special attention. She gets pebbles in her boots and slivers in her hands from the bushes which Garth and Roy, of course, are only too happy to remove for her.

As the days pass however, Garth begins to realize Linda's love of the mountains and trails is genuine and so similar to his own. She keeps close to him, as the leader and often joins him in admiring a particular view or flower. Her fearlessness appeals to him. He begins to feel impatience with Serena who makes a big production of every difficulty.

Serena senses this diminishing interest. She must be the centre of attention. It isn't enough to have Roy's. She pushes ahead to where Linda is standing on an outcropping of rock and, when no one is looking, gives her a deft push, which causes the smaller girl to lose her balance. In the fall down the slope, Linda breaks her ankle.

Roy and Serena intimate that Linda was just being clumsy and trying to get attention. Garth is furious. Though he didn't see the push, he suspects Serena of causing the accident.

Garth decides to carry Linda out to the highway by a shorter, steeper trail. In the hours that follow he can truly appreciate her patience and sense of humour, and how much they have in common.

Beyond the Next Hill

By Elsie Jean Leonhardt

Character Sketches:

Jonathan

If good looks were the criteria for a man, Jonathan Martin would have been one of the lowly. Jonathan knew he wasn't handsome, so he was spared the trouble of trying to make folks think he was.

It was the worth of a man that counted. That idea had been fed to his soul as oatmeal porridge had been to his body, and both grew big.

Discerning men saw in Jonathan, dependability and integrity. He was a man of his word. Children instinctively trusted him and brought their woes and secrets for safekeeping; and he respected them.

His eyes were vivid blue; the eyes of one who has gazed across far reaches of the prairie searching out a lost steer; up a mountain valley looking for game and across the vastness of the ocean for a sight of land.

Laughter wrinkles softened an otherwise gaunt face, and drew attention from the nose that had once been broken and the rather wide mouth.

Six foot four he stood, from his flat feet to his sandy thatch of hair, and every inch of his muscular frame betokened a hearty appetite. The broad chest tempted life-battered women to rest their heads and burdens, for just a little while.

Brought up to labor on a stony patch of land, there was little in the line of hard work he hadn't done. He had herded cattle on a ranch in the foothills, stooked grain on the prairie, felled logs on the coastal forests and worked in the mills. As faraway places called to him, he boarded and worked on steamers, and rambled through out of the way places of the world. When he had sated his curiosity about one place, he moved on to another.

Women he'd had when he wanted, they were never lacking to him, but he hadn't found one he would care to tie up to until the day he met Melissa.

Melissa

Melissa was born beautiful. Folks oohed and ahhed over her crib. She grew into blonde curly hair, big blue eyes, shaded by long curling lashes, dimpled cheeks, the whole bit. Spiteful ones reiterated "Beautiful babies grow up homely." Not Melissa. It was as if some fairy godmother had chosen her for her own.

Nor was it only curls and dimples that made her beautiful. She was endowed with a joyous nature, an inward glow. The whole world was her friend, even the crusty old mailman who detested most children, and the disillusioned policeman down the block who rarely had a good word for anyone.

Her loving nature grieved over pain and suffering. A bird with a broken wing, a battered butterfly, a tormented puppy, an abandoned kitten, all found haven in her home. When Melissa came through the door with something cradled in her arms, her mother sighed and reached for the first aid kid and an old blanket.

She wasn't overly clever at school work, but she passed from grade to grade. Perhaps it was because even the sternest teacher couldn't bear to dampen that vibrant spirit by holding her back. If she lacked in knowledge of math and physics, she more than made up for it in a questing joy of living.

Her major fault, if fault it can be labelled, was a complete trust in people. When she met Carl, she saw only the dashing good looks, and none of the coarseness, the love of easy living. She fell deeply in love.

Ten years of marriage to Carl wiped away the surface beauty, but intensified the inner quality of tenderness and loyalty.

When Jonathan saw Melissa that spring morning, he was reminded of a wounded doe he had once nursed; and his heart leaped strangely.

Story Outline:

Jonathan, of the restless feet and free spirit, is trekking north for a summer in Alaska. When the truck he is hitching a ride with pulls in at a wayside service station and restaurant, he decides to side track and look up an old crony who used to live nearby.

As he is about to leave, a plane lands neatly on a nearby landing strip. A burly man, satchel in hand, jumps out and runs for a waiting car.

"The Doc," explains the station attendant to Jonathan's query, "has to go treat a guy about ten miles out. Probably be back in about three hours so he can take off again before dark."

Jonathan trudges down the side road. When he reaches the cabin, instead of his friend, he finds Melissa and her daughter Tammy. Melissa is in severe pain and running a high fever.

Carl, her husband, had heard that gold had been found in that area. He packed their few belongings into an old truck, and had brought Melissa and Tammy to this place. Finding the cabin unoccupied, he simply took possession. As a result of puttering around in the cold water of the creek, trying ineptly to pan gold, he had taken pneumonia and died.

Melissa had gotten help to bury him nearby. She now hasn't any money, the truck has broken down, and now she has suddenly become ill.

Jonathan knows enough about sickness to realize Melissa needs medical help, and soon. He suddenly remembers Doc's plane and his imminent return. Melissa must be taken to it before Doc takes off.

Could he get the old truck running? The tires are poor, but inflated. The gas gauge stands almost on empty but it might make it to the landing strip. He sets to work on the truck, improvising all he can. On the last life of the weak battery, the motor springs to a roar, and he eases the vehicle up to the door. Melissa is gently placed inside, Tammy next to her.

The ancient truck coughs and sputters, but keeps going. One of the tires goes flat. Jonathan breathes a prayer that the spare will hold. As he comes over the hill leading down to the landing strip, the gas gives out. As the car coasts down the hill, Jonathan can see Doc's car swing into the hangar. Jonathan presses frantically on the horn.

Doc is starting the motor, will he hear? As the old truck turns in at a field, Jonathan jumps out and runs toward the plane.

The plane starts taxiing down the runway; then swings back. In so doing, Doc sees Jonathan waving wildly and brings the plane to a halt. Quickly he climbs down as Jonathan carries Melissa over to the plane. Doc deftly checks her over, then carefully places her in a stretcher on the plane. Jonathan and Tammy crawl aboard and they take off for the city hospital.

It is a year before Jonathan visits Alaska, but he does return, it is to show his favourite views to an appreciative wife and daughter.

To Each His Own

By Elsie Jean Leonhardt

Old Josh hated women. He'd been married once, a long time back, to a sharp tongued shrew who had bossed him within an inch of his life. Then one day she took off with another man, taking their pale, thin daughter with her. Josh was so glad to see her go, he didn't begrudge losing Belinda. He had heard that Martha had died, and supposed she was busy bossing the angels now; probably that was why the weather had been so unpredictable lately.

Anyhow, he lived in peace now, let his whiskers grow into a fine beard and moustache. When haircuts went up over seventy five cents he let his hair grow too, so that now he had a flowing white mane. His bright blue eyes twinkled under bushy eyebrows.

He kept house to suit himself, swept the floor so he could get around in sock feet, made the bed so it wasn't lumpy; ate when he felt like it and did the dishes when he ran out of clean ones. When his socks got holes in them, he turned them over and wore out the top part. Clothes got washed when he went to town, and he had rigged up a shower to sluice the dirt off himself every evening.

Old Josh had a way with animals, a healing touch. Not an animal in the valley was ailing but he was asked to come treat it.

Digger, the mongrel, who had come to his door more dead than alive, was his constant companion and his vicious bark kept most women away. There was usually an orphan lamb or weak piglet snugged away behind the stove. A squirrel Josh had rescued from a trap, had a nook behind the old clock on the shelf.

Old Josh was at peace with his world, until Amanda entered it...

Amanda Wright was well past middle-age when she came to the valley. She had been an obedient daughter, subservient to a strong minded mother until death took over with a stronger hand. Amanda had then tenderly nursed her gentle father until he eased out of life.

Some quirk of fate plunged into her marriage. Was it insecurity or simply a need to be needed?

Pete had no home of his own, so they lived in the home she had inherited from her parents. He was always ailing when there was work to do, but able to beg for money from her small inheritance. She kept the farm going rather than dip into her small savings. Whenever she threatened Pete with a divorce, he'd pull his bad heart stunt.

Pete departed his life, not from a failing heart but from a combination of high speed, alcohol, and a too ardent hold on the pretty young waitress he was escorting to a secluded cabin. She was thrown clear when the car rolled, but there wasn't much left of Pete.

Amanda went home from the funeral and tossed her sensible black hat in the fire. She sold the house and farm, gave away her staid sensible clothes and the old furniture.

She bought a compact trailer, a good used car, some smart new clothes, got her first permanent and a colour rinse in her greying brown hair. Then she took the open highway, singing in her rich contralto. Her brown eyes sparkled with adventure and her determined little chin lifted in a new independence.

Some two thousand miles from her old home, she pulled off on an attractive side road, and discovered a delightful weatherbeaten farmhouse for sale. Here Amanda settled. She bought some sheep, a cow, some chickens and adopted a little black kitten which grew into an enormous black tomcat. Though her home was only a mile from Old Josh's, she didn't meet him until the day Little Bess, her jersey cow needed help.

Amanda has been in the valley five years. She has heard of Old Josh's eccentricity regarding women and feels a sympathy and respect for him. Live and let live is her motto. She has been told of his almost miraculous way with sick animals, so when Little Bess is having difficulty having her calf, Amanda calls Old Josh.

Though brusque with her, he is tender and efficient with Little Bess, and soon delivers a lovely calf.

When Old Tom breaks a leg in an encounter with a speeding car, Josh is called again. The big black cat recovers and becomes very attached to the old man.

Amanda hears from the storekeeper, that Doc has been out to see Old Josh. The old man has pneumonia from sitting out nursing a new colt. "Pity he won't have a nurse come in," says Mr. Barker. "That old coot's too stubborn to go to the hospital. Don't know what will become of him."

Remembering Josh's tender touch on Little Bess and Old Tom, Amanda gathers up items she needs for nursing, goes up to the hitherto forbidden territory.

Digger, sensing her purpose, wags his tail at her. Ignoring Old Josh's rebuffs and insults, she quietly settles in to care for him. After she and old Doc pull him through the sickness, he wakes one afternoon to find her sitting by his bed darning his socks. The house is neat and cheerful. Chipper the squirrel is on her shoulder tweaking at her hair. Old Digger is snoring at her feet.

"Traitors," he snorts. Then he sees Tom snuggled up on his bed, purring like a buzz-saw.

As soon as he's able to be up, Amanda leaves. Josh misses her but won't admit it. After several days he wonders why she doesn't call. Then he recalls that the last day Amanda was there, she had looked troubled and as if she had been crying. Just like a woman.

He notices some strange young men driving up and down the road. Then, one day Mr. Barker calls in for a game of checkers. He tells the old man that the government is putting a highway through Amanda's place, and have bought her out. They are going to start working and insist she move. She is terribly upset as she can't find another place in the valley.

Josh is surprised at the turmoil of his feelings. Finally he goes down to see Amanda and convinces her they should "get hitched". After

all, it would be an awful shame to break up
Digger, Tom and Chipper.

For Unto Us a Child is Born

By Elsie Jean Leonhardt

Marie, an immigrant mother is about to give birth to her sixth child on Christmas Eve, on a homestead in southern Alberta.

It has been a very difficult year on the homestead. There has been very little with which to feed and clothe the five children they already have. She had been dismayed in the spring to find she carried yet another child and had tried to dislodge it from her by heavy work, but the baby has clung tenaciously.

In the fall, her husband, Henry, had gone to work in the mines to make a living for the family. An accident in the mine seriously injured him and he was taken to a distant hospital. She has had no news of him, and concludes he has died and the family fear to tell her because of the imminent birth of the child.

As the labour begins, in the late afternoon before Christmas, Marie puts into motion the plans she has been making. She sends the children to her sister's shanty a mile distant on the prairie, so they can join in the Christmas Eve festivities there. Arthur, the eldest, is reluctant to leave her, but she tells him he must care for the others, especially little Katrina, hardly more than a baby herself. Reluctantly, he leaves with the others who are excitedly talking about Christmas. The children all have dark eyes and hair like their mother, which was a disappointment to their tall blonde father, who complained that "a man should be seen in his children."

Marie plans to birth the child alone, then snuff out its life and present it as a stillborn. She hopes that it will be stillborn, but if not, she will do what she feels she must. She feel she cannot bring up yet another child without Henry.

The birth is more difficult than she had anticipated. As the pains rack her she remembers other Christmas Eves; her home in the German settlement along the Volga, how she longs to be there once more; of their betrothal, and their wedding the following Christmas Eve. She feels again the agony and loss of their first child, born prematurely at sea while they were emigrating to America.

Pictures of the difficult, but happy life they shared in the American city where they had lived and four of their children had been born, pass before her closed eyes.

She remembers her first sight of the homestead in the Canadian West, which Henry and his brothers had taken so they could have land of their very own, lots of good land. She chuckles in spite of her pain, for Henry, instead of building a shanty on the flat plains above as the other homesteaders did, had built a cozy shelter into the steep banks bordering the river. The one wall with door and windows faced the south, so the sun shone warm upon it summer and winter. And nearby, like at home, was a cave sheltering the cows and horses. So close were they that she could hear their stirring and the occasional bawl or snort.

She rouses herself to sterilize the scissors, the same ones she herself used when she was called upon to assist her stepmother in her last delivery. The scissors had come with Marie to the new land and had already been used five times to separate new lives from her.

As the birth is now imminent she puts lumps of coal, dug from a nearby bank, upon the glowing coals in the stove and turns up the lamp wick for more light.

At last, the time comes and she brings forth the child. It is alive, a husky boy child. She severs and ties the cord, the babe squalls lustily in seeming fury of being thrust from its warm nest into a cold world.

Weakly she tries to bring herself to quench its life. Startled, she draws back the pillow, for the light seems to cast a nimbus about the head. It is fair, not dark like the others were.

She wipes it carefully with a soft cloth. A blonde fuzz covers the tiny, perfectly shaped head. The unfocused eyes gaze upwards at her. She clutches the infant to her, knowing she cannot take its life.

In sheer exhaustion, she falls back upon the bed, and puts the babe to her breasts. As its tiny lips clutch at the nipple and draw the first drops of nourishment, the resentment she has carried with the child, ebbs away.

As if in a dream, she hears happy voices outside. The door is pushed open and, with the sweep of cold air, Henry strides into the room. He is followed closely by Arthur and the doctor, whom the boy had walked to fetch for his mother, after leaving the other children safely with his aunt.
The doctor had just returned home from the city with Henry. Arthur had met them and told of his concern for his mother.

Henry's joy is unbounded, to at last have a son, like himself, but he's also very proud of his eldest son who has been the man of the family for so long....

Notes from Elsie:

The setting for the foregoing story is a cave, a homestead shelter in central Alberta, in the early years of the century.

The story encompasses the late afternoon and evening hours of the day before Christmas.

In the flashback scenes I hope to show Marie, the mother, as a woman conditioned by her environment to face the reality and hardship of homestead life. She has not a hard and selfish nature, on the contrary she is a loving wife and mother. She's overcome by the strangeness and loneliness of this new land, and she feels she must take this action for the good of her other children.

The Luck O' the Irish

By Elsie Jean Leonhardt

When Nate O'Dwyer set up a new still in a well concealed nook on his bush farm, he had no way of knowing that he was setting in motion a train of events that would jeopardize his comfortable way of living, and change ours.

Uncle Nate, as he was known to everyone in our bushland backcountry, was a local character. He had an Irishman's dislike for authority; and a liking for a good joke and good whiskey. When the latter became difficult to obtain, he started to make his own, and his neighbor's supply; a practice frowned upon by the local constabulary.

Uncle Nate live comfortably alone in his little shanty, which also served as a retreat for all the local men. It was the ideal place to escape from female domination for a few hours.

He was small and wiry with bandy legs and keen blue eyes brightened by a fringe of white hair standing out around a bald dome. Since he was a jack of all trades, he was the local handyman. Men liked having him around because of his endless store of jokes & bawdy songs.

Women, though suspecting and disapproving of his whiskey making, melted under his winning Irish flattery, and rivalled with each other to win his praise for their cooking.

My mother had a distinct advantage over the other women; she was a first-rate cook, but she was also a beauty straight from the Ould sod, and a widow. With no man around the farm, she had innumerable odd jobs that needed Uncle Nate's special talents.

She had one definite disadvantage however, me; a twelve-year-old imp of Satan who could inevitably be found where there was mischief. I had dashed her matrimonial hopes on several previous occasions. Uncle Nate however, seemed to be more wary of her than of me, and took me unequivocally under his wing.

Neighborhood children hung about him, because he always had time to hear their troubles and to tell them stories of leprechauns and the "little people". I idolized him, and many a time he got me off the hook when my mother came after me with fire in her blue eyes and hair brush in her capable hand.

*   *   *   *   *   *   *

A revival and temperance meeting is being held in the neighborhood Gospel Church. My friend Bucky Harris and I plan to play some tricks on the people gathered there. We decide it would be great fun to remove the buggy wheels. Tramp, Bucky's dog, tags along after us.

Bucky's dad has his supply of Uncle Nate's "remedy" stored in the barn. Unknown to Mr. Harris, we have taken a mischievous delight in giving nips from the jug to Tramp, who has developed quite a taste for it.

We cut through Uncle Nate's field following a well-defined path. Another faint path branches off towards a tree covered bluff. Tramp runs down this one and begins to snuffle and scratch under some bushes. We think he's after some small animal and decide to stop and help him. After a little scuffling of the vines and dirt, we find the entrance to a cave. Exploring further, we discover Uncle Nate's still and store room. We decide to try this new batch to see if it's as good as Mr. Harris's.

Bucky, Tramp and I do quite a bit of "sampling" from the jugs before we decide to get on with the planned pranks. Somehow the ground doesn't seem as steady beneath our feet as it did when we came in, but we continue in the general direction of the church.

Arriving at our destination we decide that as our hands aren't quite coordinated for removing nuts from buggy wheels, we will join the meeting.

Uncle Nate is sitting at the back of the church lustily singing "Strong drink is full of pain and woe, and I will never touch it." The air from the overheated room strikes us as we enter, and brings about very undesirable effects. Despite my misery, I see Nate slip out the door and I suddenly feel deserted.

Consternation and confusion reign. The Gospel team are very indignant and try to use the spectacle to strengthen their arguments, but our mothers are intent only on getting their errant sons home.

When I wake up the next morning, I have one gigantic hangover. When my mother sees I am all right otherwise, she pins on her hat, dons her good coat, and I catch her surreptitiously putting on a little makeup and a dab of perfume.

Though I never rightly heard the story of my mother's visit with Uncle Nate, for neither was inclined to mention it for a long time, the gist of it seemed to be, that her son needed a father to keep him out of trouble. If Uncle Nate would kindly undertake that job, all legal and such, there be no need for her to observe her civic duty and guide the Mounties to that little cave back in his field.

A week after the incident Ma and Nate get married and settle down on her farm. When the going gets a little rough, "Dad" and I slip back to the old shanty for a little peace and quiet, and discussion on the ways of "wimmin".

The Blizzard

By Elsie Jean Leonhardt

Eighteen year old Cathy Grant is teaching school on the prairie. She is young, pretty and idealistic but lacks confidence and is easily discouraged.

The homesteaders in this district are puritanical and demanding. They criticize her harshly and undermine her authority over the children by their disparagement.

There's one exception, a widower Keith Robson, whose six-year old crippled daughter attends school. Cathy has become very attached to the little girl, Laurie, who is so cheerful and patient despite her disability, a twisted foot which makes walking very difficult.

Keith stops by each afternoon to pick up Lori, to give her a ride home on his horse. He has been pausing to talk to Cathy for a while many evenings, and she has found him to be a quiet, thoughtful, intelligent and well-educated man.

In the other children, Cathy sees the parents. As she looks at Jane for instance, she sees the acid-tongued mother who sharply reprimanded her for using a little makeup. In Rena, she sees the mother who accused her of smoking "because all city girls smoke." Jack's mother is a gossip who had maliciously whispered the information that the teacher preceding her had been "in trouble" when she left. "It was that widower that did it too."

In Andy's bold eyes and constant trouble making, she sees the father who had attempted to rape her one day after school. When she threatens to report him, he retorts that no one would believe her; after all he is an elder in the rural church and chairman of the school board. He warns her she had better cooperate and be "good" to him or else. Only the arrival of Keith had saved her that time, but she wonders what she's going to do to prevent another attack. She realizes that this is what happened to the former teacher.

She feels that her work at the school is useless, but she needs the money. Can she finish the school term, she wonders. The situation has become critical and one winter afternoon as she is pondering the situation, a blinding blizzard strikes the little schoolhouse.

Prairie trails lead to the school and these will soon be obliterated in the terrific wind. There's only one fence leading from the school to a dwelling and it is North, straight into the wind and blinding snow. Could they possibly get to it? She realizes Laurie certainly couldn't, even if she and the others could. They will have to stay at the school until the storm abates.

As Cathy and the children work together to spend the night at the school, she begins to see the children as individuals instead of duplicates of their parents.

The boys bringing blankets and quilts from the buggies and pails of coal from the shed. They tell her the alarming news that there's only a little coal left and it is mostly dust.

Hunger is a problem. The lunches are barely adequate for dinner for the hungry children. Andy slips up to Cathy and asks if she can cook a rabbit. He caught one in the school barn and says he can skin and dress it "if'n she kin cook it." She finds the pot used for making coffee at the school gatherings and is thankful for the recent "salt and flour" projects. The rabbit stew proves quite appetizing.

Cathy organizes active games to keep the children warmed and their minds off the howling of the wind. They sing songs and she tells them stories as they sit around the stove. Then she has each of the children tell her about his or her life and home. As they eagerly tell their stories she just discerns minds that are eager for learning, heart starved for affection, and souls being twisted by the fanatical ravings of a series of pulpit-pounding itinerant preachers. Cathy realizes now that they have been looking to her for help and once again sees the purpose for her teaching.

Throughout the long night they come to a new understanding of each other. The boys realize she is a "good scout" and the girls reveal a shy admiration for her dresses and appearance.

The blizzard eases off at dawn and as the last pail of coal burns off, Cathy ponders what she can use for the fire when a group of parents arrive. She finds she can look at them through new ways of thinking and can understand a little better the reason for their narrow mindedness. She neither likes nor trusts Andy's father but she resolves to give him no opportunity to see her alone.

The parents, also, seem to see Cathy in a new light and praise her handling of the situation. They seem anxious now to accept her as one of them.

Later she rides to her boarding house with Keith and Lori, he asks if she will consider changing her job next June. Though she anticipates her teaching will be much more enjoyable now, Keith's suggestion has much more appeal.

Love Comes in Curious Ways

By Elsie Jean Leonhardt

Dunc McTavish had been an only child, born to middle aged parents to whom work and saving money had vied with God as their deity. These principles had ruled and overshadowed their son's childhood. When Mr. and Mrs. McTavish passed away in Dunc's early manhood, they left him a debt-free and prospering ranch, but little knowledge of the pleasures of life.

Most of the matrimonially-intentioned young teachers who had come to the local country school considered Dunc "a catch". He was young and handsome in a rugged way but so painfully shy with girls that the young ladies had ultimately settled for other local young men. As they became young matrons however, they turned to matchmaking, intent on getting Dunc a wife.

Melissa Davies was different; she took her teaching career seriously. When she came to the school she seemed dedicated to helping her pupils widen their horizons not only in school studies, but in many fields of endeavour. She spent many extra hours teaching music and handicrafts. Interested students were treated to trips to the city to visit museums and attend concerts with her. Melissa was especially interested in sports, however, and encouraged the young folks to participate by arranging tournaments with other schools and giving parties where sports were emphasized and discussed.

Dunc, accustomed to evading predatory females, is somewhat surprised at Melissa's complete dedication to her work. During her first year at the little school, Melissa and Dunc cagily assess each other and when she returns for the second year he begins to make tentative overtures. He enters the local stampede – the one field of competition he is familiar with and excels in. However, Melissa is unimpressed – she finds it barbarous and sympathizes with the animals who are being ridden and thrown.

The young rancher longs to join in with the activities Melissa arranges but feels shy and awkward. Finally he is encouraged by the avid matchmakers to attend a skating party Melissa is giving. True, he has never been on skates, but he has broken bucking horses to ride, ridden steers, and branded and handled cattle from the time he was ten, so why should skating be a problem?

In a spirit of recklessness, he purchases a pair of skates and sets out for the pond. En route, he stops at the local veterinary office for a tube of some red dye he needs the next day for marking his calves. This he places in his shirt pocket.

As he puts on his new skates, Dunc begins to feel a few qualms about this venture, but as he tries to think of a good excuse to leave, his joshing friends out-talk him. The sight of Melissa gracefully skating with her city boyfriend, however, and this young man's derisive remarks about local cowboys, eggs him on more than the encouragement of the local youths.

At first, he manages not too badly, really. But suddenly a small child careens toward him in fun, expecting Dunc to dodge him. When he cannot, the child plunges into him upsetting the young man's already precarious balance, and sending him into a series of contortions in an effort to regain balance. The tube of paint becomes dislodged from the open pocket and falls to the ice to be closely followed by Dunc. As luck would have it, his head cracks sharply on the tube, breaking it open and spilling the scarlet contents.

Melissa's indifference vanishes; Dunc is a creature in need and she flies to his aid, thinking he must be badly injured. He is taken to the teacherage and the doctor called, despite Dunc's protests. When it is realized that it is the dye that caused the alarm, Melissa is very annoyed and feels she has been made to look a fool. Then remarks by her urban friend and Dunc's extreme embarrassment make her realize his deeper need for her concern and the emotional ice between them is broken.

Note from Elsie:
This is story outline only. The initial crises would be Dunc's extreme reserve where girls are concerned, and his need and yearning to overcome this. The climax would come in his attempt to prove himself by skating when he has never been on skates in his life.

Mother and the Salesman

By Elsie Jean Leonhardt

Mother was a whistler. She whistled while she scrubbed, and baked, and canned. The whistle rose above the krr-whump of the treadle sewing machine and the thumps she gave the bread dough.

Dad loved tinkering. As a result, Mother had the first washing machine in the district, a weird and wonderful contraption. Set in motion it clanked, clattered and roared; but it worked, and every Monday morning, Mother's strong clear whistle rose above it.

The tunes she whistled were the barometer of her pressures: patriotic - high spirits; hymns - low spirits. If she started "Rock of Ages" we knew the towels were tangling in the wringer. "Beulah Land" meant one of them had ripped.

The magazine salesman wasn't as perceptive. As he climbed out of his dilapidated "lizzy", Mother's whistle came to his ears like an angel's hallelujah. Why not, after confronting the acid tongues of the ladies doing their wash via the scrub board?

His ancient suit hung loosely on his gaunt frame, so no doubt the aroma of the washday stew bolstered his optimism also.
He jauntily approached the wash house door just as Mother launched into "Oh Darkest Woe".

In this story opener, the reader is aware of information that the characters are not. The salesman does not realize that Mother's tunes are indicative of her mood and Mother does not realize there is a salesman on her doorstep. Write what you think will happen when the salesman and Mother come face to face.

The Trap

By Elsie Jean Leonhardt

Little waves borne on the breath of a light breeze rolled up on the sandy beach, touching Janice's brown toes. She curled them under with a shiver of delight, but held her huddled body quiet otherwise. Her thin brown arms were wrapped around her scratched knees, and her cheek rested against them with long braids falling forward.

"If I sit very very still," she mused.

Earlier that afternoon, Janice had fled the tense troubled atmosphere of her home and had again sought the peace and solace of her favourite haunt.

"Why can't they be honest with me?" she stormed at the jay high in the old pine tree, "And let me be honest," she added sadly. Then she laughed a little as the jay scolded back at her, a woodpecker cocked his head on one side for a minute, then went back rat-a-ta-tatting. Now, she sat in fetal position on the shore of the small lake. She had a fragile elusive quality that blended strangely with the quality of the late summer day. Autumn was just a whisper away for both. Little waves borne on the breath of a light breeze rolled up on the sandy beach caressing her toes.

Soothed by the lap of the waves, the rustle of the drying leaves and woodland scents, she drew strength unto herself. From this vantage point she had on several occasions watched a doe and two fawns…

When I was transcribing Elsie's stories, I discovered the above gem and was heartbroken to only have the first page in my possession. I have many questions about Janice, her past and what my grandma planned for her. Please use this piece as a story starter and continue the story.

Tornado

By Elsie Jean Leonhardt

Uncanny silence pressed heavily on the land, undulating under the brassy sky.

Halfway down a row of corn, Grace Lattimer straightened and rested wearily against the hoe. Despite the stifling heat, a chill crawled up her spine and raised the hair on her neck. Rags, the sheepdog, padded up and whined uneasily as he pressed against her.

"Gramps," Grace called to the old man, painstakingly staking tomato plants at the end of the garden, "what does your rheumatism tell you about this weather?"

The old man removed his straw hat and swept his wispy hair with a faded red hanky. Before he could reply, a little blue-jeaned figure came flying from the barn, braids bouncing against her bare shoulders.

"Mommy, Sadie's hid her kitties again. Do I have to weed? Can't I look for them?" Her pixie face, wet with perspiration, suddenly looked troubled. "Mommy! Gramps!" she shrieked. "Look at that cloud!"

With her last words, the tension spring that held all nature suspended, snapped. A funnel shaped cloud hovered in the northwest. A low roar rose out of silence.

"Grace, Jinny," Gramps came running, "the root cellar, quick! No! Not the house, the root cellar!"

A good story needs a captivating beginning to hook the reader. Try writing your own hooks or write the rest of "Tornado".

www.ingramcontent.com/pod-product-compliance
Lightning Source LLC
Chambersburg PA
CBHW021933170626
46807CB00007B/3086